Little Red Riding Hood

illustrated by Jess Stockham

Child's Play (International) Ltd
Swindon   Auburn ME   Sydney
© 2004 Child's Play (International) Ltd   Printed in China
ISBN 0-85953-675-0 (h/c)   ISBN 1-904550-22-3 (s/c)
3579108642
www.childs-play.com

"I thought I'd go and visit Grandmother today," said Little Red Riding Hood.
"That's a good idea," replied her mother.
"Why don't you take her a basket of treats? She has been sick, and they will cheer her up. Be careful walking through the wood. There may be wolves!"

Little Red Riding Hood loaded the basket with lots of lovely things. "I'll put some apples in as well," she thought, and picked some shiny red ones from the tree. But she didn't realise that a hungry wolf was watching everything she did.

The wolf jumped out in front of Little Red Riding Hood as she skipped through the forest. "Don't come near me," she warned him. "Or I'll shout for Will the Woodman!" "I only wondered where you were going," answered the wolf. "To see my Grandmother," Little Red Riding Hood explained. "And no, you can't come as well. Off you go!"

The wolf slunk back into the bushes. Little Red Riding Hood went on her way, but in the middle of the wood, she stopped to make a daisy chain for her Grandmother. The wolf, meantime, ran ahead to Grandmother's house, and climbed in through an open window. But someone was watching him...

"Please don't eat me," begged Grandmother.
"I'm only skin and bone, not a nice meal at all!"
"Don't worry!" snarled the wolf. "I'm after fresher meat!"

He tied poor Grandmother up,
and shut her in a big cupboard.

As soon as he had shut Grandmother away,
the wolf went to her wardrobe.
He took out a big nightdress and put it on.
Then he put on her best nightcap
and her glasses, and jumped into bed.

Little Red Riding Hood found her Grandmother
tucked up in bed. "I'm a bit better now,"
said Grandmother in a husky voice.
"But it's lovely to see you anyway."
"You look a little different,"
said Little Red Riding Hood, peering at her.

"What big eyes you've got!"
"All the better to see your pretty face with," replied her Grandmother.

"I've never thought this before,"
said Little Red Riding Hood, peering closer.
"But what big ears you've got, as well!"
"All the better to hear your sweet voice,"
answered Grandmother.

"And I hope you don't mind me saying,"
said Little Red Riding Hood, peering very closely
indeed. "But what big teeth you've got!"
"All the better to eat you with!" snarled the wolf
as he jumped out of bed,
tore off his nightclothes,
and leapt at the little girl.

But before he reached Little Red Riding Hood,
Will the Woodman burst through the door.
The wolf took one look at Will's axe, and fainted.

"Where's Grandmother?"
said Little Red Riding Hood.
"And what's that banging from the cupboard?"
Will opened the cupboard door,
and Grandmother rolled out onto the floor.

Little Red Riding Hood put her Grandmother back to bed, and together they shared the basket of treats with Will.
"It's quite a party,"
said Grandmother.
"I'm feeling better already!"